Also by Satoshi Kitamura:

Igor, the Bird Who Couldn't Sing

Me and My Cat?

Pablo the Artist

Sheep in Wolves' Clothing

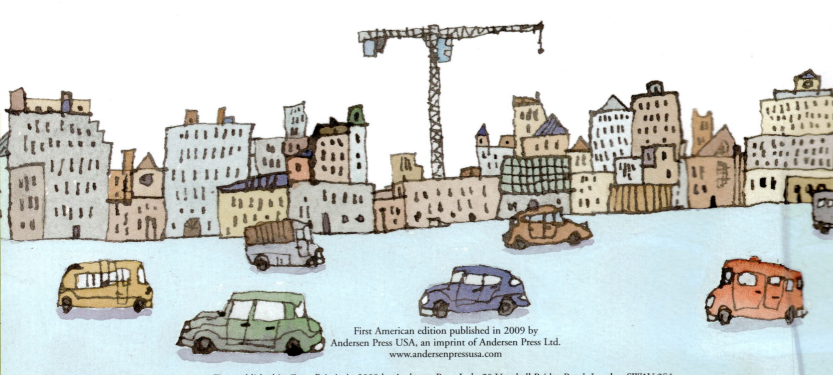

First American edition published in 2009 by
Andersen Press USA, an imprint of Andersen Press Ltd.
www.andersenpressusa.com

First published in Great Britain in 2009 by Andersen Press Ltd., 20 Vauxhall Bridge Road, London SW1V 2SA.
Published in Australia by Random House Australia Pty., Level 3, 100 Pacific Highway, North Sydney, NSW 2060.
Copyright © Satoshi Kitamura, 2009.
The author and the artist assert the moral right to be identified as author and artist of this work.

Distributed in the United States and Canada by
Lerner Publishing Group, Inc.
241 First Avenue North
Minneapolis, MN 55401 U.S.A.
www.lernerbooks.com

Library of Congress Cataloging-in-Publication Data Available.
ISBN: 978-0-7613-5153-5

Manufactured in Singapore.

1 2 3 4 5 6 - 14 13 12 11 10 09

Millie's
Marvellous
Hat

Satoshi Kitamura

Andersen Press USA

Millie was walking home from school when she came across a hat shop.
There were lots of hats in the window, but the one she liked best was the one with the colorful feathers.

Millie went inside.

"May I see the hat with the colorful feathers, please?"
she asked the man behind the counter.
"Certainly, Madam," replied the man, and he fetched the hat
from the window.
Millie tried it on. It suited her perfectly.
"I'll take it," she said.
"An excellent choice, Madam," said the man. "That will be
five hundred and ninety-nine dollars and ninety-nine cents."

Millie opened her purse and looked inside.
"Oh, dear," she said. "Do you have anything a little cheaper?"
"What sort of price were you thinking of, Madam?"
asked the man kindly.
"Well . . . about this much," said Millie and showed him her
purse. It was empty.
"I see . . ." muttered the man, and he looked up at the ceiling.
Millie looked up at the ceiling too. It was covered with
interesting patterns.

"Aha!" said the man suddenly. "I think I have just the thing for you, Madam. Wait here a moment, please."
And away he went to the back of the shop.
A few minutes later he returned with a box in his hands.
He placed it on a table and removed the lid.

"This is a most marvellous hat, Madam," said the man.
"It can be any size, shape or color you wish. All you have to do is imagine it."

Carefully, the man took the hat out of the box and put it on Millie's head. It fitted her perfectly.

"Thank you," said Millie, "I like it very much!" She put her hand in her purse and handed the man all she had in it.

"Thank you, Madam," said the man. "Would you like your hat in its box?"

"No, thank you," said Millie, "I'll take it just as it is."

Millie felt happy in her new hat.
"But now I must think what my hat
is going to look like," she thought.
"Perhaps it has lots of feathers like
the one in the shop window,

only even more feathers . . ."

It was a peacock hat!

Millie stopped outside a cake shop
and looked in the window.
All the cakes looked delicious.

So Millie had a cake hat!

When Millie passed a flower shop
her hat became flowery . . .

. . . and in the park she wore a fountain hat!

Suddenly Millie saw that she was not the only one with a special hat . . .

Everyone had a hat of their own. And they were all different.

She saw an old lady
who was wearing a dark, murky pond hat.
Millie smiled at her and
the birds and the fish leapt out of
Millie's hat and onto the old lady's.

Millie felt like singing.

And so did her hat.

By the time Millie arrived back home, her hat had grown so tall that she couldn't walk through the door!

So she thought of another hat . . .

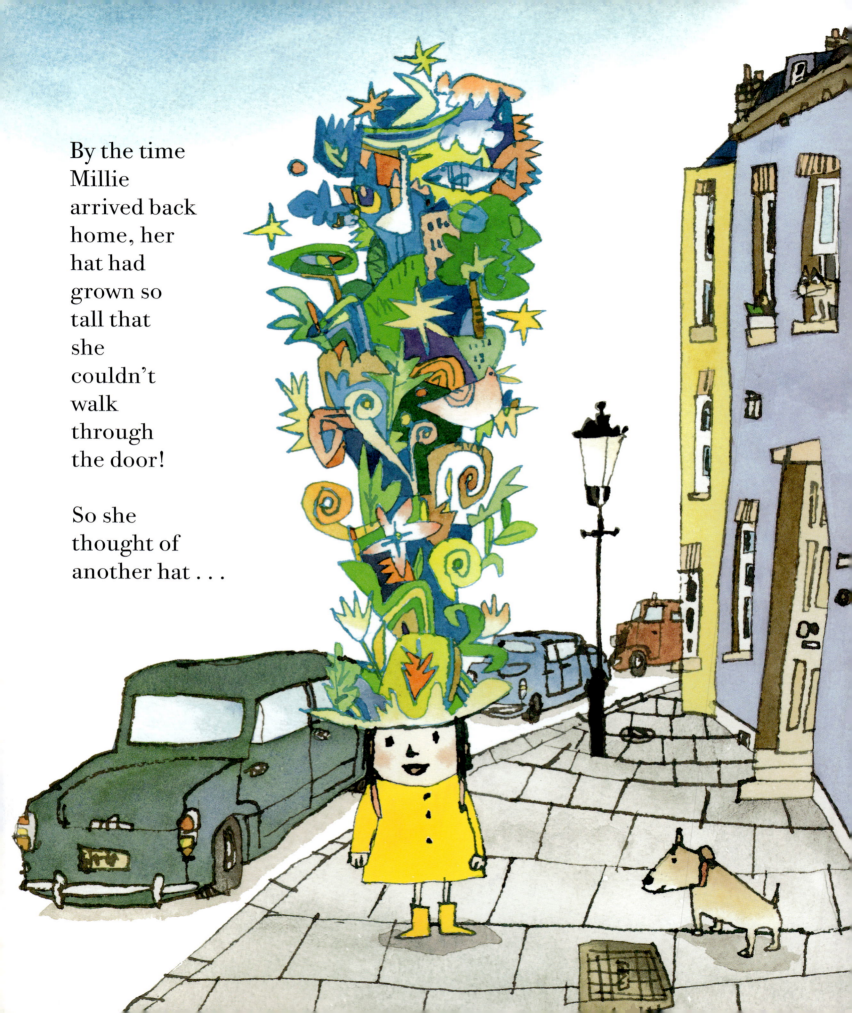

"How do you like my new hat?"
she asked when she saw her mum and dad.
"New hat?" said her mum. "But you haven't . . ."
Then she stopped and smiled. "It's a marvellous hat, Millie.
I wish I had one too."
"But you do have one," said Millie. "You only have to imagine it!"

And she was right.
Everyone has their very own marvellous hat.